D0938190

Sir Cassie to the Rescue

This book is dedicated to Luke, Stephen, Josh and Emily, who over the years have kept my childhood alive with their imaginative play.
LS

To Brontë, Lachlan and McDuff.
KP

National Library of Canada Cataloguing in Publication Data
Smith, Linda, 1949-

Sir Cassie to the rescue / Linda Smith ; Karen Patkau, illustrations.

ISBN 1-55143-243-9

I. Patkau, Karen. II. Title.

PS8587.M5528S44 2003 jC813'.54 C2003-910451-6

PZ7.S65425Si 2003

First published in the United States, 2003

Library of Congress Control Number: 2003103893

Summary: When Cassie reads a story about knights and damsels in distress, she wants to act it out, but she can't get anyone to play the damsel.

Teachers' guide available from Orca Book Publishers.

Orca Book Publishers gratefully acknowledges the support of its publishing programs provided by the following agencies: the Department of Canadian Heritage, the Canada Council for the Arts, and the British Columbia Arts Council.

Design by Karen Patkau
Printed and bound in Hong Kong

Orca Book Publishers
1030 North Park Street
Victoria, BC Canada
V8T 1C6

Orca Book Publishers
PO Box 468
Custer, WA USA
98240-0468

05 04 03 • 5 4 3 2 1

Sir Cassie to the Rescue

written by Linda Smith
illustrated by Karen Patkau

Orca Book Publishers

Cassie read a story about knights.

An evil knight grabbed Lady Veronica. He locked her up in his castle.

Sir Thomas rode to the rescue. He slew the evil knight and freed Lady Veronica.

"Oh, thank you!" cried Lady Veronica. "You are a true, brave knight."

Cassie closed the book. She thought for a minute. Then she went to find Trevor.

“Let’s play knights,” Cassie said.

“What do knights do?” Trevor asked.

“They live in castles, ride horses and rescue damsels in distress.”

“All right,” Trevor said.

Cassie and Trevor built a castle.

It had high walls and a wide moat.

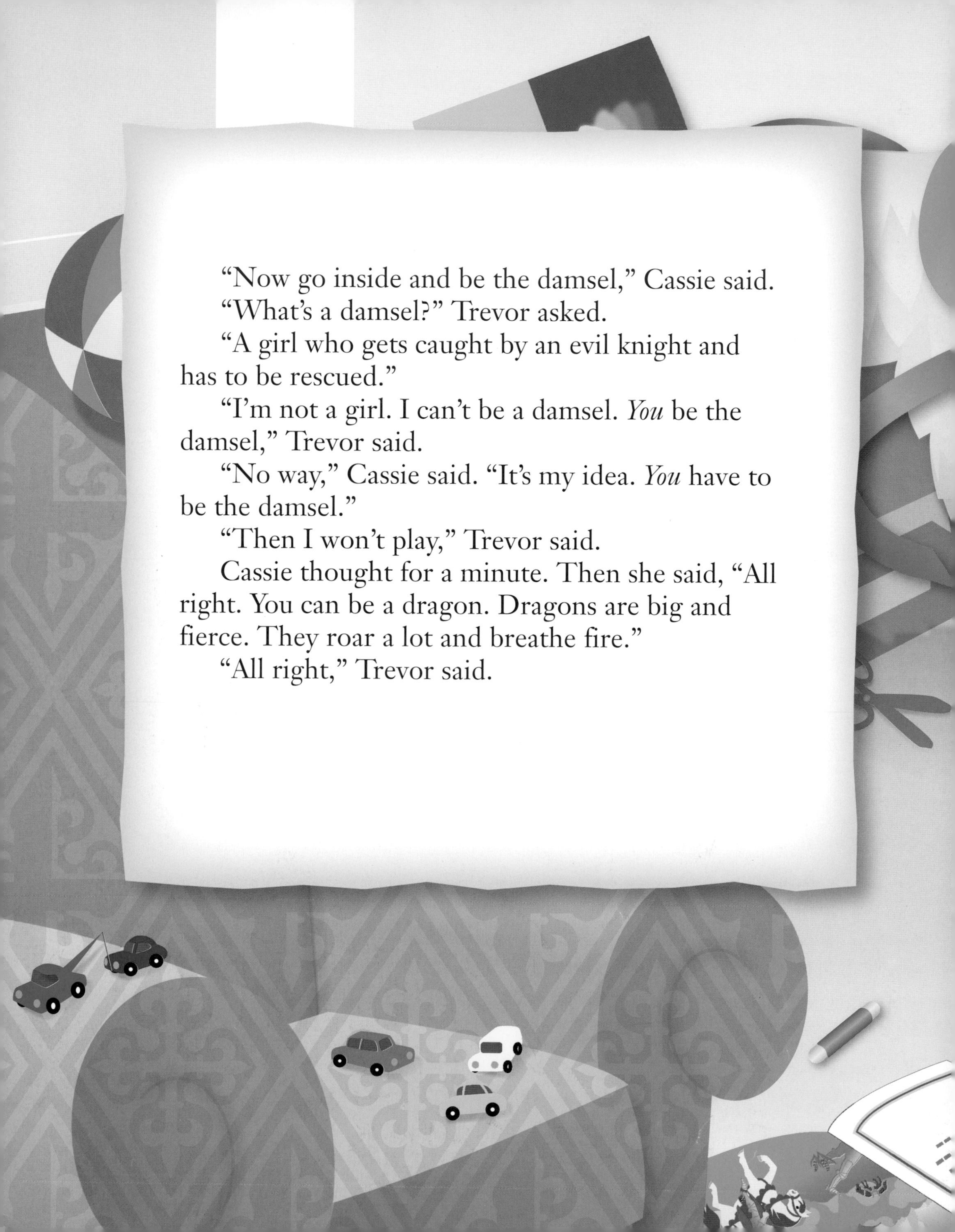

“Now go inside and be the damsel,” Cassie said.

“What’s a damsel?” Trevor asked.

“A girl who gets caught by an evil knight and has to be rescued.”

“I’m not a girl. I can’t be a damsel. *You* be the damsel,” Trevor said.

“No way,” Cassie said. “It’s my idea. *You* have to be the damsel.”

“Then I won’t play,” Trevor said.

Cassie thought for a minute. Then she said, “All right. You can be a dragon. Dragons are big and fierce. They roar a lot and breathe fire.”

“All right,” Trevor said.

Cassie and Trevor built a cave.

They filled it full of treasures for the dragon to guard.

The dragon was very fierce. He rushed at Sir Cassie. Sir Cassie fought bravely. She stuck the dragon with her sword, but the dragon refused to die.

"You have to die," Sir Cassie said.

"Why?" asked the dragon. "I'm big and fierce." He roared to show how big and fierce he was.

The queen appeared in the doorway. “Be quiet. Amanda’s having a nap.”

When she had gone, Cassie whispered, “You have to die because that’s what dragons do.”

“Then I won’t play,” Trevor said.

Cassie thought for a minute. Then she said, “All right. We’ll both be knights. Towser can be the dragon.”

Towser liked being a dragon. He especially liked jumping on the knights and licking them with his fiery breath. But he refused to die too. He preferred chasing the knights round and round and roaring.

The queen came back. She looked cross. “You’ve woken Amanda. Now you’ll have to look after her while I get lunch.”

Cassie looked at Amanda. She thought for a minute. Then she said, “Amanda can be the damsel in distress. We’ll take turns being the good knight and the evil knight. I get to be the good knight first.”

“All right,” Trevor said.

Cassie and Trevor built another castle.

It had higher walls and a wider moat.

Sir Cassie charged the evil knight. The evil knight fought back. The damsel in distress clapped and cheered. She even tried to help by knocking down the castle walls.

Cassie and Trevor built a new castle.

It had even *higher* walls and an even *wider* moat.

Sir Cassie was the evil knight this time. The good knight ran at her. Sir Cassie fought and fought. She wouldn't give in until the dragon jumped on her.

The damsel in distress got tired of waiting to be rescued. She knocked down the rear wall of the castle and crawled off into the forest.

"Time for the battle to end and all knights to come to the feast," said the queen.

It was a great feast. The knights, the damsel and the dragon all thought so. Then the queen ordered the knights to clean up the castles and the cave. It took them a long time. When they had finished, Cassie decided to read another book.

She thought for a minute. Then she picked up a story about pirates.